READINGS
IN THE
SHED

READINGS IN THE SHED

NIKHIL KATARA & HIMALI KOTHARI

PARTRIDGE

To order additional copies of this book, contact
Partridge India
000 800 919 0634 (Call Free)
+91 000 80091 90634 (Outside India)
orders.india@partridgepublishing.com

www.partridgepublishing.com/india

"Until I feared I would lose it, I never loved to read. One does not love breathing."
~Harper Lee

CONTENTS

PREFACE

Pedro Paramo by Juan Rulfo is buried somewhere in this book which has stories by Nikhil Katara and Himali Kothari. It is a book I admire greatly, and anyone who has read Pedro Paramo can well crawl into bed and die.

I have known Nikhil Katara and Himali Kothari as theatre-practitioners and hosts of Readings in the Shed for the past three years. I've seen them evolve as artists, developing an assured voice and building an audience for their work over a period of time.

I have been on the jury in which Nikhil Katara's play *Castling* was in the reckoning for The Hindu Playwright Award, which is a prestigious national-level award.

For more than three years now, Katara and Kothari have tried to create work as theatre-maker, both directing and collaborating, as well as writing plays. The work at Readings in the Shed travels from nation to nation, looking at the important voices as a site of literature, protest and high prose. Some of it gets reflected in the words in these stories.

Nikhil Katara's story *Pride* is a quest for humanity in the 21st century. He deploys the Disney animation metaphor of beasts and wild animals to make sense of mankind. In O_2, Nikhil Katara looks at a heightened and complicated relationship in the Covid world. The story is set in a typical Mumbai upper-class house. The varied perspectives are illuminated by the crisis of the Covid calamity. It creates a deathly choice at the end and becomes a motif for the complete collapse of the medical healthcare system in the new shiny India.

Himali Kothari's work looks inward. Her story is populated with characters who are drawn from a mix of people she knows. The Birthday Stories looks at the terrain of sexuality and questions of identity. Even though the characters are familiar, the story reinforces the universal theme of friendship. Then there is the story of Pushpa, who worked long hours as a daughter in law in her new home - not knowing her date of birth. As time passes, her life is reduced to emptiness. A doctor came to the house to assess Pushpa and advised her to stay in bed. The point Kothari makes is, is Pushpa too unimportant to survive Covid?

I compliment Himali Kothari and Nikhil Katara on the publication of Readings in the Shed. All the best for more.

By Ramu Ramanathan;
Kharvel Village

FOREWORD

Readings in the shed was launched in April 2018, with the intent to bring, to the stage, stories from different parts of the world. Stories that carry the culture, the ethos and traits of their place of birth. The performances are designed to enable the audience to travel to those regions and experience its flavours and at the same time, get a sense of universal resonance.

The text for the performances is driven by the subject matter of the reading. The subject may be based on a local or global concern that needs to be highlighted or it may be based on topics that lend to conversation. The origin text for the performance may be in the form of short stories, essays, letters, excerpts, plays, newspaper articles...any form.

Next, the text is made stage-ready. This could involve creating original scripts of editing the original text, without compromising its integrity. Simultaneously, a light scheme is developed. A soundscape is planned with live or recorded music. Images are sourced to create projections to accentuate the setting of the story. Objects that carry meaning in the story are identified to be placed in the performance area. All this helps the audience to inhabit the world of the story for the time they spend in the Shed.

Theatre artists are engaged to perform the text and multiple rehearsals are carried out to ensure that the performers are familiar with the words and the layout of the space of by D-day.

In the pre-pandemic times, Readings in the Shed presented events on a monthly basis at established auditoriums, libraries, art galleries, restaurants, schools, outdoor venues…any space that was large enough to accommodate a reader and his script. During the pandemic times, the readings carried on through the online and video format.

This book is a collection of short stories by Nikhil Katara and Himali Kothari to commemorate the third year of Readings in the Shed.

No matter what transpires in the universe, the day the stories stop, the apocalypse will be imminent.

To all those who read with us

NIKHIL KATARA

On one fine morning a decade and a half ago, Nikhil woke up from the right side of the bed and decided to write a play. He wrote about all the fine philosophies that his mind could think of and eventually came up with a script. It had the answers to every existential question that one could encounter. Now since the work had been written, someone had to produce it. He looked for people to produce, but couldn't find them. So he decided to produce it himself.

That play happened, and things began to change. The answers that he was so confident about, had more questions that challenged it. He studied Philosophy at the University of Mumbai and got introduced to the works of Kant, Heidegger, Camus, Sartre, & Dostoevsky. He found meaning in their books and many others. He started a reading group that has been reading and critiquing classic and contemporary literature on a weekly basis and found many inspiring people there. They read together, and discussed together.

On another fine morning on 23rd April 2018, he founded the initiative Readings in the Shed that performed all sorts of stories every month. He performs and directs them, and now, three years have passed. The questions still remain, but they are sometimes answered on stage by some author or poet who lives in the words they have written.

Pride

CHAPTER I

Being a lion is serious business, and there are no Happy Birthdays

What was that smell? Cape buffalo? No, it couldn't be; this smelled more dry. A rhinoceros, maybe? No, he'd catch that scent easily. Maybe this was a zebra. Old? Haggard? Near death? His mouth watered. Never does food come and present itself that easily. He crept like the shadow, moving swiftly one step after another. It was breezy; his mane, now speckled with age, could feel it. The wind was telling him where to go. His paws gravitated towards the smell. He had to be careful, his paws were no longer as strong as they used to be, and of course, there were others around. Others that could smell it too. The younger, swifter, and quicker others. But they were not him, and they had little knowledge of how to bring prey down with ease. A moment passed, and then another, nothing happened. Slowly he reached the baobab. Its wide trunk stood invitingly. What was that old legend? Yes, the giant child of the old Gods had ripped the baobab out of the ground and replanted it upside down. Maybe that's why it looked like that. Maybe that's why it could hide a full-grown lion behind it with such ease.

'But enough talking, there he is. That old thing, standing, waiting, wishing for a swift end maybe. But where is Satan when you need him? Do I have to do all of this alone? The Gods have presented a full meal near us, and he has decided to take a walk… Why do I have to do this work alone when…'

Satan zipped past him. It took only a moment for him to realise what had happened. He had raced on, moved like the wind. Satan was younger, but he would not be left behind. He leapt and latched on. The wind was behind; that always helped. But Satan was ahead now, and when he was ahead, no one could find a way to go around. He breathed in, out, in, out, faster, faster, faster. He stopped. It was already over. Satan had held the feeble old thing by the neck. Everything was silent.

Snap.

There goes the spine. The zebra gave a last gasp before falling to the ground. The body convulsed, and death came. Satan stood over toweringly.

"Happy Birthday Shaka." He said.

"Are you mocking me?"

"I am wishing you. It is the day you were born, and today you deserve to take the first bite."

"I was ready to take it on alone, who asked you to creep..."

"How old are you today?"

"I am 9..."

"Liar... I am 9; you must be twelve."

"So I am. How does that change anything?"

"You have become slower. There was a time when you had..."

"Time changes everything, my friend; you'll get to where I am soon. But there was something very funny about this prey here."

"What?" Satan stood looking at it.

"See. The leg has been wounded, and there are bite marks already."

"That means?"

"It means someone had attacked it and left it here. Now, why would someone do that?"

"I think you are overthinking."

"This is the jungle, Satan; you better start overthinking before your gut is torn and open for hyenas to feed."

"What are you trying to say?"

"This is bait. We're in a trap. Guards up…"

They looked around, north, south, east and west; they were surrounded. The last light of the day was on them; as the trees shivered, their rustles could be heard from the distance. Their branches swaying in the wind. The ground around them was sloping, but it was evident that in all four corners in the distances, they could see the lions staring back.

Roar!

They walked and came forward. They did not attack. They were coming to talk. But maybe they were also coming to tell them who owns these lands. If things didn't go as planned, anything could happen.

Shaka considered the moment. It had happened many times before; how many? A hundred lions, their cubs, their females? How many had come, and how many had died? Five more…

The one who came from the North looked familiar. 'Asad is it? That big old thing? No, this one is slightly smaller but looks exactly like Asad. My old big brother.' Shaka thought.

At least he pretended to be. But Shaka remembered what the others did-not. Asad was never a part of the pride. He was a smart lion, a cunning lion, a lion who knew how to make a place for himself. The real Asad was dead and gone when he was all but twenty-one months old. He had seen it himself. No one comes back from the mouth of the hyenas when you are that young. Asad had gone and come back. But not the same one, the one who came back was bigger, stronger, and smelled different. He was an impostor, but no one had the guts to fight off a big lion, least of all the ones who wanted to live. The new Asad never left and grew to be a leader. A place that was rightfully his.

But the five lions who had come together in the rule of Asad had been the force of the jungle. No lion lived while they were around. Asad, Zuba, Jacob, Shaka and Satan could break the back of every pride and kill every cub that breathed. It was him and Satan who'd usually start things and finish them too. Asad ruled for no reason. He didn't deserve to rule. Maybe that is why…

"Thanks for killing the zebra off. You saved us the trouble. You're new here?" The lion, who looked like Asad, spoke. He didn't look like a leader at all. But the females made do with what they have until someone better came along. Shaka licked his lip and said…

"Yes. What about you?"

"You are in our territory."

"We are? I don't think you've marked it well enough; maybe we should teach them how to do it, Satan?" Satan gave a slight smile and a nod.

"I am Unika from the Malane tribe; here are my brothers Namib, Zahara, & Armani, and that is Kodjo. We ask you to leave the lands. We will give you one chance."

"And what about this meal that we hunted?"

"All of it belongs to us, and if you don't go, you will leave us with no option."

"Unika, I give you a counteroffer. You leave and let us eat our meal in peace, and once you do that, you might live for today. Any more interference, and we'll kill the five of you right here, right now. Now that would be a great birthday gift Satan," Satan roared.

"You have the audacity to challenge us in our lands. Who are you?"

"We are Shaka and Satan from the Mago lion coalition. We have lived our lives fighting cats like you. Now let's cut the talking short. Are you going back to where you came from, or would you like to die? Let's not waste time."

The roar of Namib echoed. He was evidently the aggressor; Zahara followed, and then Armani; they were not going to back off too. Unika roared the loudest, seemed like permission for the others to attack, but what about little Kodjo? He took a step back. He was scared, was he? Ahh! Shaka thought. He is the one.

"To the little one, Satan."

They leapt and ran together. Satan and Shaka went north, the other lions came behind, but the small one was taking some time to understand what was happening. He was not moving.

'This is simpler than I thought'. Shaka could see fear in the cub's eye. Big mistake, big, big mistake by Unika. You never get such a young one to hunt. The old lions enjoy this. Tables turn very easily, and little effort does it take. He could hear Unika from behind.

"Kodjo, Kodjo go, go, go…"

But Kodjo didn't move a muscle. Fear is it? It does strange things to lions. Shaka had not felt such fear before, but he had seen it. It was always in the eyes, the animal could do nothing but wait, and Kodjo was waiting, unmoving, waiting for death to come.

In a flash, he was on Kodjo. Satan was not too far behind. Shaka held him by the throat, small throat it was, easily holdable. Satan waited at the back. The throat tasted weak; if this were how the throats of the Malane tribe were, then they would have a tough time. The weakest branch of the baobab seemed to be stronger than this little one.

Unika and his tribe arrived but held back.

"Wait," Unika said. "You must not harm him."

Shaka released the cub, who fell in a daze. As he tried to run back, Satan got him by the neck again. Shaka watched with a wry smile.

"I like how the aggression weakens when it comes to the little ones. Don't worry; after we're done with all of you, we will find your females, kill your other cubs, and maybe give birth to new ones. The ones who are lion enough."

Unika seemed like he was holding back. This lion seems to be special; what about him makes him so special? Shaka wondered. Maybe he was an important figure in the tribe. This big congregation of lions are protecting this cub, is it? How about that? Shaka thought, maybe it was a good time to make a deal.

"How about you have a deal with us? We leave your little cub, and you leave these lands? Now onwards, we will rule the North, and you can migrate?"

"That can never happen" Namib reacted to it almost immediately

"This is our home," Zahara spoke almost simultaneously

"Unika, don't fall into their trap," Armani followed.

Unika considered the offer for a moment. "You assure us that you will let Kodjo go?"

"Yes," Shaka replied

"You assure us you will not harm a single cub in the vicinity."

"Yes"

"You assure us you will not lay your dirty paws on the Malane tribe females."

"I assure you," Shaka replied

Satan let go of Kodjo's neck and spoke, "Why would you assure them that? We will need females to build our tribe?"

"You do not have the permission to speak when I am negotiating." Shaka roared.

"I do not agree on these conditions. We need the females, and we will kill everyone until we get them."

The Malane tribe roared together.

"We will find females."

"No, we won't."

"Stop this immaturity."

"I have heard enough of you" Satan went towards Kodjo, held his neck and…

SNAP!

Silence!

The lion fell limp to the ground. Blood dripped from Satan's mouth, and Unika, Namib, Zahara, and Armani stared in shocked silence.

"Oh, Satan! What have you done? We had won without fighting," Shaka said.

"What is the point of that win?"

The fierce roars of the Malane echoed through the distance. They would attack anytime.

"We can't fight all four of them together. We have to find cover." Shaka said. In the distance, he could see the magic guarri. They were dense shrubs that covered the lands for many kilometres. They would give them the chance they need.

"To the bushes," Shaka said, and he was off.

CHAPTER II

The run was quick. Shaka hadn't run that fast in a long time. Even Satan was left behind. He could not afford to get caught by the Malane tribe. He could hear them in the distance. Running. Roaring. Reeling. They were losing ground. He turned and changed direction. From the corner of his eye, he could see Satan do the same. This would make them lose the pursuit altogether. But it was only a few metres before they could run that he felt a paw hit him in the ribs. That hurt. He fell to the ground holding the wounded flesh, now oozing with blood.

There were no Malane around. It was Satan.

"Have you lost your mind?" Shaka roared.

"I had. Now I have understood." Satan replied.

"What have you understood? How to kill your brother?'

"You are making me weak. We have never run away..."

"Four of them are chasing us. They are hungry for revenge...'

"And each of them deserves to die like that other cat who is now a meal for the hyenas. Why are you scared, Shaka?"

"I am not scared. I just wanted to take them one at a time. You need to understand that we can kill all of them only if you strategise and don't behave like a..."

"Lion?"

"You are a fool."

"No, you are one. I remember, do you think I can ever forget how you tricked the old lion. You never had it in you. You could never lead. Asad knew, and he knew you would cheat him. He knew you would..."

"Stop this instance."

"We'd brought down a giraffe. Asad had led us. I remember it was the first big kill of the year. But you, you wanted to bring him down. You wanted to lead the coalition."

"It was my right to..."

"You could not stand in front of him. Your attacks, your attempts to fight were..." Satan laughed.

"Why are you with me then? Why did you leave Asad?"

"Because I wanted to be with you. We'd fought together. Always. But today."

"Today?"

"Today, you are nothing. You are running away from a bunch of..."

"I am protecting you."

"I am Satan from the Mago lion coalition. I am a lion. No one needs to protect me."

"You are a fool. Come with me if you want to live."

"I will come for you after I am done with them. Run while you have the strength."

Shaka walked away. He wanted to leave, but something slowed down his steps. He knew they were coming. Their smell was rife in the air. Shaka kept walking until he found a small hole in the ground. He wanted to get away, but he stopped. He halted to see Satan.

He went under a pile of fallen leaves and waited. Satan was visible. Quiet. Contemplative. He made no sounds, just licked his paws as if preparing for the battle that was about to begin.

One after another, they came. Silence. Not one said a word, but all their gazes were fixed on Satan. He looked back. The silence was deafening.

They began to roar. One after the other, the jungle was filled with their voices. In the distance Shaka noticed another animal unlike any other he had ever seen. It rolled into the lands and stood waiting as if watching what was about to occur. It had strange eyes that glowed. As if it were made from light itself. But in its belly, smaller things stood and watched. They were gorillas or baboons; he could not tell. All he could see was that they stood on two legs. The belly of the giant creature soon started to flash like lightning. One after the other, the apes lit the sky with flashes and then it all went dark again. Except the eyes of the creature. They always glowed.

Shaka turned his gaze towards the lions. The Malane were fixated on Satan. With no warning. With not even a word, Unika leapt. A cloud of dust broke out as the others followed. Roaring and growling, the lions were on their move. It was war. The four attacked together. Mercilessly. Two of them went for the hind legs, and two went for the front ones. They pinned Satan down. A paw, then another went for the soft underbelly as he shrieked. Shaka watched in disbelief. The flashes from the distance came more often now.

It was a while before Satan could move, but in a desperate effort, he freed himself and stood up. The four moved away. They were angry, but they were no fools. Defence. They seemed to have a plan. Shaka understood what it was. If he attacks, he is vulnerable. He will tire soon. If he defends, he will be overpowered by their numbers. There was little Satan could do. He needed help. Maybe he doesn't realise it. Shaka knew when to go for the attack and when to defend. To fight a powerful enemy is suicide; to not go with a plan is arrogance. If he went to help, he'd die.

But Satan, being Satan, attacked. He went straight for Zahara's jugular and caught him. Unika, Namib and Armani went for the back immediately. Zahara was losing consciousness. Satan didn't let go. The others kept pawing and biting until fresh wounds oozing with blood developed.

In a brief few minutes it was over. Zahara was dead.

"Two down, three to go," Satan said and smiled.

The three lions roared together in one big giant roar.

He needs help. Shaka could see it. He needed help. He lifted his legs as he crept out of the leaves.

He walked towards them.

One step. He saw them pin Satan down again.

Second step. They were biting into him.

Third step. Armani and Namib held him.

Stop.

Unika ripped into Satan. Shaka could move no further. Satan, the lion who looked like he was made of metal, was now hollow.

What was this feeling inside him? This strange bile that grew. Was this fear? Was Satan right? Shaka had lost all ability to fight back. There was a deep hollowness inside him. Something that took him back. He could see the giant paws of the lions in front of him. He could see their menacing eyes. He could feel the angry roars, and it chilled his blood and his veins.

A step back. He saw them going for the spine now.

Two steps. They bit into it together.

Three steps. Blood dripped from their mouth.

Stop.

Snap.

They broke his spine. Satan fell limp on the floor.

Shaka couldn't explain that feeling. The moment he heard the bone break. His eyes widened. The memories flashed like the flashes emerging from the monster's belly. Flash. Teaching Satan to attack from the back. Flash. Moving noiselessly towards prey. Flash. Walking on the new lands together for the first time. Flash. Licking each other's wounds.

The night was almost lightless, except the eyes of the monster and the flashes that emerged from it. The wind cascaded down towards Shaka. He breathed the air in, and looked upwards. The baobab, the bushwillow and the magic guarri rustled as if speaking of the events that had just occurred. The moon emerged in the night sky. The clouds moved away to reveal the ghost of the night. It looked like death itself. The earth sat in quiet stillness, embracing Satan. He looked calm now. He breathed heavily. A small ribbon-like road separated him from his brother. There was nothing he could do. His legs didn't permit him to walk.

The final blows came in still silence. The night had turned colder. Frosty. Satan's body came apart. A body that had torn into hundreds of hyenas, buffaloes, lions big and small was now a pile of nothing. It did not breathe. It did not fight. It did not move. The blood now everywhere drenched the earth, and in the distance, the lappet-faced vulture hovered quietly, waiting for the lions to leave.

The hyenas, too, were here. The filthy animals, waiting for what was left of Satan. After the lions were done with him, they would come. The forest left nothing. The carnivore, the herbivore. The plant, the bird and the bees were all brought down to one simple truth. Food.

He saw the lions now move away from the body. They quietly went towards the body of their own dead brother and lowered their heads. Perhaps telling him that a part of the revenge was taken. They then moved on, never looking back, never turning around. Maybe they knew that the scavengers were around, but that is the law of the jungle.

Shaka walked towards his own dead brother. The hiding and the waiting had almost paralysed his legs. The fear still made his body tremble. The images returned. The flashes and the scent. The scent of the remains of his dead brother made him weak in the limbs, but he moved on. He had to see him one last time. He had to pay his respects.

Satan's eyes still seemed to be alive. They looked like they always looked, this time into the sky. "I will come for you after I am done with them", he had said. But that wasn't meant to be. Shaka lowered his head. This was the day he was born. It was also the day his brother died. Why should this day be remembered? He thought.

As he passed the body of Zahara he looked at him for a moment too. By what instinct he could not tell, he lowered his head. In the distance, he could hear the forest respond. The hyenas, the vultures, even the small little insects. 'The loss of someone is gain for the other. Many must not have eaten for days, and this fight between lions has yielded enough food for a week.'

Shaka walked on, but after walking for, what seemed like some time, he looked back. He saw the hyenas had arrived, and they were aplenty. They didn't wait but immediately went for it. They had powerful jaws that could break the thigh of a buffalo in one bite. Some of them could feed a third of their weight in one feed alone. When they would be done, not much of the two lions would remain. The lappet-faced vulture had descended from the skies too. He could tear through muscle and hide. It was looking at the dead remains of the animals and the celebration of the hyenas, perhaps wondering where to start from or waiting for the hyenas to get done.

Shaka turned around and moved ahead with many thoughts in his mind. One thing was for certain, that the Malane's wouldn't let him be. They would not stop until he was either dead or gone. The other thing was also for certain. He could not let this go. He could not let them walk away after this humiliation. But how could he fight this newfound fear in his body? How could he fight three lions so much bigger and younger than him? How could he take revenge and live to tell the tale?

CHAPTER III

Shaka stood near them. Eleven bodies. Eleven cubs lay in front of him. He stared at them with calm. The job was done. A little in the distance lay Armani. Quietly looking at the lioness near him, breathing his last. With difficulty, the words "Run Jabari" left him. Death came. She kept looking at him, though. Broken. Distraught. Destroyed.

"Death is a strange thing, isn't it?" Shaka said as he approached her.

She stumbled onto the ground, barely able to articulate herself. "Why did you do it?"

"Revenge. The cycle of revenge. Your tribe killed my brother."

"And you killed eleven cubs and Armani in return?"

"Not eleven. Twelve cubs. Zahara and Armani. Now only Unika and Namib remain. I will get them soon too."

"May the mother protect them."

"It was their choice. They came to us. They brought their little boy Kodjo. They challenged us. We were bound to fight for honour."

"Kodjo was not from here."

Shaka thought about it. What had just been said? They had fought for so long.

"Too much blood has spilt for a lion who didn't even belong to you."

"It was an oath."

"What oath?"

"The lion had come to ask for help. In our tribe, if someone comes for help, we swear by the Old Gods to protect them. Our own was protected by another when he was lost. But you won't understand."

He approached Jabari and went closer. She didn't move back. "I promise you, when this is over, we will start anew. Don't worry; I am not going to hurt you."

"You say this now? When you've killed everyone?"

"I have to, that is what I was born to do. To rule."

"Let's see how long you rule for without the lionesses."

"Where are all the others?"

"They are on their hunt. You must pray they don't come back soon because once they do, you will have to deal with them. I promise you; they will destroy all of you in less than a minute."

"I take your word for it. But I don't intend to fight them. They are my pride now."

"I think you don't understand the rules of the lands you walk on. Let me make it clear. They will never accept you. I will never accept you. Your death is near."

He couldn't stand the sight of her. How dare she even try to dissuade him? She'd do the same to the other lionesses. She might influence them. That would just be an impediment to his plans. Perhaps having her was not the best idea. Perhaps living wasn't the best option for her either. He went for her throat and bit into it. It was an instinct he could not suppress. What was this? A bloodlust? Was killing her necessary? What was happening to him?

Soon it was over. She lay near the many bodies. To kill so many and live to tell the tale. That is what he wanted. But why wasn't he feeling the pride of the conqueror yet? Maybe because the job wasn't over? Maybe because he was always under threat until Unika and Namib were breathing. This had to end for a new beginning.

He leapt into the magic guarri and found a knob-thorn. Its crown was full with the yellow flowers of spring. It wasn't as big as the baobab, but it would do. He waited. Unika & Namib may come anytime now. They might see their dead and understand what had happened. Perhaps they'd lose their mind after that, wouldn't they? He had seen that happen many times. The loss of one cub was hard; the loss of so many could not be imagined. They'd go in all directions, attacking the first living thing they saw. A lion in this state is dangerous. A lion in this frame of mind is also vulnerable. He isn't looking. He isn't thinking and cannot predict what is about to come. That would be his chance.

The leaves rustled again as he heard paws silently moving towards where the dead lay. His breath became slower. He tended to breathe silently in times like these. From the distance, he couldn't see them, but he most definitely could hear them. Paws, one after the other, stepping onto the ground. Paws, one after the other, walking towards their doom. Paws, one after another, stopping. Silence.

Their voices. As expected. Turned to growls. Wild running. Stopping. Roaring. It all happened together. It was very hard to see, but it was very easy to feel. Shaka could hear the madness on the other side of the bush. Shaka could feel the pandemonium. They were lost. They were disturbed. They were going to die. He could not help but smirk.

But they were coming right at him. Fear. The dreaded fear returned. In their madness, they were running in his direction. The fear grew like an orb inside his stomach. He was no match for them; he knew it. They would tear into him by brute strength alone. He needed time; he needed a strategy; he needed them to go in the other direction. Could they smell him? Thoughts, fear, and madness had made room inside his heart now. He could not move. He could hear more than two now. Three lions? Who was the third? Someone new had just arrived. There were measured steps on the ground. Whoever had just come wasn't going wild. He was walking slowly; he knew what he was doing. This was not going according to plan. The knob thorn was a bad idea. It was not going to help him. He had to run. But if he did, he would be vulnerable. But before he could decide to race or pounce a face emerged.

Shaka took a moment to recognise him. This was not Namib; he was fairly bigger than that. He was not Unika too; this lion was older, bigger, stronger. It was Asad.

"Come out," Asad spoke.

Shaka obeyed. His legs were entrenched into the bushes and took a while to emerge, but he walked slowly and glared into the eyes of the two other lions in the distance, pacing, looking. Unika and Namib caught sight of him and charged. Asad stood in the middle, and they stopped.

"Are you going to protect him?" Unika said.

"I would like to understand how this happened?" Asad spoke.

"I have no time for explanations," Namib went towards Shaka, and Asad stopped him mid-way. He was no match for Asad.

"Where is Kodjo? Zahara?" asked Asad.

"They are dead," Unika spoke after a moment of reflection.

"What happened?"

"From the day these two arrived till today, we have lost everyone."

"And Satan?"

"He is dead too. These two killed him in front of my eyes," said Shaka.

"Oh! Do you know what you have done?"

"I have done what had to be done," Shaka said.

"And we will have to finish this," Unika replied.

"You will have to know the true nature of things before you continue this bloodbath. Shaka and Satan are my brothers. He is a part of that pride I went into when I was separated from you. I thought I had lost you when the hyenas attacked. It wasn't that they attacked our pride alone. They had attacked the Magos as well, and in that, the lion who died was like me. I thought I would never be able to see you and the others again. So I went and became a part of the *Mago Lion Coalition*. For many years we challenged the hierarchy of the forest. We even stood and fought the big five- we fed on the buffaloes, the rhinoceros was wary of us, the leopard never entered our territory, no lions challenged us, and if they did, they never left alive, and even the royal elephant, the ruler of the lands, thought twice before getting into a scuffle with us. We had the power to rule for many years and gave birth to many cubs. But the coalition split when Shaka attacked me. I knew he would someday. I knew he hated me because he was the only one who knew that I was not born in the pride. But the day it happened, he ran away, taking Satan with him. Time went by, and we lost Zuba and Jacob. The cubs grew and looked up to me. Some of them asked me questions about the coalition. Why was it lost? Why were the hyenas attacking us and not scared anymore? I had no answers. I needed more lions. So I took one of them and left to search for Shaka and Satan. That's when I met you, Unika. From the moment I saw you, I understood that I was wrong all these years. I had never lost you'll."

"And that's when you left Kodjo with us and went on in your search," Unika spoke.

"I thought it was a way for him to be safe."

"We couldn't, Asad. We couldn't keep our promise to keep him safe."

"Kodjo was from our pride?" Shaka asked.

"Kodjo was your son," Asad replied.

That moment came back to Shaka. That moment when he had leapt onto the little lion who looked at him with those familiar eyes. Perhaps he had no fear in them. But hope. Perhaps he'd realised who Shaka was. Maybe he was looking forward to meeting his father. He'd travelled all the way up north to speak to that lion who had left, and he had taken the cub's throat in his mouth. It was soft and weak. Satan had broken it with such ease. Death, the truth of the forest, which comes every day in different forms. Had come and gone so easily. Shaka, while planning all his strategies, knew nothing.

"Satan and I killed our own cub?" Shaka spoke finally.

"You did." Said Asad.

"And we killed your brother, Asad." Spoke Unika

"And now I see many more dead here."

"I killed them. I killed them all." Shaka said, unable to make sense of what had happened. The face of Kodjo returned to him as he spoke.

The moment stood heavily on Shaka. He could see Unika and Namib looking at Asad and then at the dead bodies around them. Perhaps they were asking for permission to let them take their revenge. Perhaps they wanted to kill Shaka before the lionesses returned from the hunt to feed no one.

Asad finally moved towards Shaka and spoke. "I had come to meet you and take you back. I had come to ask you to join the pride again. But after what you've done, no lion can trust you again."

"So you are going to let them kill me?" Shaka asked.

"I have to do it myself," Asad said.

He looked Asad in the eye. It was what he had to do. To look at the brother he once had. To look at the leader, he once followed. To look at his own death staring right back at him.

Unika and Namib walked towards their own dead and lowered their heads silently. They walked on, not looking back. It seemed it was all over for them. Asad walked towards Shaka and lowered his head. Shaka noticed the old lion's mane. What had begun on the day of his birth was going to end on the day of his death. The cycle was complete; at least it was complete for him. Asad would live on, but for how long? Perhaps not too long. He had far exceeded the days a lion could live. Maybe he would succumb too, soon. Maybe they'd meet in the afterlife, with all the others they'd hunted with, with all the others they'd killed, and the forest on the other side of death would be a kinder, less harsh place. By instinct, Shaka, too, lowered his head. This was his chance to pay his respect.

"I trust you will make it quick."

"I will."

Shaka saw Asad move towards him. He felt his paws on him. There was no fear this time. Just the quiet of the forest breaking into a wind that spoke to him in the ear. It was a warm embrace, which got tighter and tighter. He could see the sky go dim. In the distance, there was the baobab. What was that old legend again? Yes, the giant child of the Old Gods had ripped the baobab out of the ground and replanted it upside down.

But in the real world, the royal elephant was trying to eat its bark. He could see the grace with which the king was reaching for the tree. Just a small touch of the trunk and the Baobab came crashing down. Heaps of fibre lay everywhere. Death had come to the tree and looked swift and immediate. That massive tree was planted by the child of the Old Gods. That tree which had roots going deep into the Earth was dead so swiftly? Shaka noticed that it was hollow from the inside. Maybe it was hollowing for many years. Maybe the royal elephant was just the means to an end which was anyway going to come.

The magic guarri was quiet as slowly sleep came. Shaka felt no pain, he felt nothing. The last sound he heard was the roar of a lion, and in the distance, he saw a baobab. It was right side up, unlike any baobab he'd ever seen. He walked into the new forest without looking back. It was time.

O-2

A Monologue

Ravi: Thirty-four years old, holding a file and prescriptions.

This monologue should be performed after taking permission from an audience member to be a part of it. The audience member should sit on a chair, and the actor must maintain a six feet distance from him/her at all times.

Ravi: It all starts with a position, a point of no return. A decision. Which one has to make. We all have to make decisions, don't we? I dread that word. Sometimes we make decisions for ourselves, sometimes for others. Sometimes we have decisions enforced upon us. Other times we enforce them ourselves. It all goes around in circles. But it isn't so easy to make one, is it? Think about it… Doing the thing we do? Being who we are is not really easy, and no matter what we believe in, what faith we have, and whatever thoughts keep hitting our mind, sometimes we have to pause and consider our position. Our point of deliberation.

What can I do?

What will I do?

If you are wondering why did I jump in and start this elaborate conversation on decisions. Let me tell you my intention right at the onset. I had to make a decision one day, and I still wonder if my decision was the right one. Will you help me figure it out?

But for that, you need to know who I am, and so I would like to introduce myself in no uncertain terms. You see, until you don't know my story... My entire story, you will not be able to help me, and you also need to understand that even I don't know my entire story. For example, I have no recollection of the day I was born and also of the few years, I spent growing up. My most vivid memory is from when I was four years old. But I don't remember anything before that, and I really can't say with conviction that what I am going to tell you now about myself is going to be enough for you to help me in any way. But if I don't even try to speak to you and tell you my story, you will have no idea how to help me. So... No matter how flawed it is... No matter how unreliable my capabilities are... and no matter how less or more things are communicated between you and me, here is my attempt...

They call me Ravi... No... Just Ravi... I don't have nicknames, and I don't like to be called anything else but Ravi. I was born in Mumbai to a Sindhi community. Do you know who Sindhis are? They were originally from Sindh, which now lies in Pakistan. We have our own script, our own language... You must have heard it many times, or maybe not; it depends from which part of the globe you are. So from what I remember, my ancestors came from that part of the world where many Indians want to send many other Indians when they disagree with each other.

Yes! That's true. My great grandfather had one day decided to pack his bags and shift to Mumbai, then Bombay, and relocate his entire family here. I bet that was a tough time, and I bet he had tough decisions to make. But I am glad I was not in his position because I don't know what I would have done.

My earliest memory of how life was, is fuzzy. I remember having a television at my beck and call. You see, I was never an active kid. I loved to lie down and watch the television until it ran out of shows. I also had my video games. The video games that I used to love were Mario... Contra and of course my favourite one... The duck hunt. You remember that? A bird would move around the television screen, and you had a gun in your hand, and when you would shoot the duck, it would actually fall inside the screen. Then a dog would run in and fetch the duck. Of course, this excited me. What do you expect? I was so young. This was my equivalent to a Nintendo Wii or the Xbox. It was insane.

But apart from playing the games on television, I had no company. I was the only child in a world of adults. No one, absolutely no small person for kilometres. There were all kinds of adults, though. You know my mother, who would be so busy cooking food all day, she had no time whatsoever. My father, who was so busy doing business dealings all day, had no time whatsoever. My grandfather, who was busy handling legal cases all day, had no time whatsoever, and of course, there was my grandmother, who also had no time whatsoever.

Do you know how it is to grow up in that environment? Like having no one who is around you who can tell you, Hey, why don't you come out for a game of cricket, or Hey! Why don't we go out cycling, or Hey! Let's just play some football. I didn't play sports when I was growing up; it wasn't for me. I mean, other kids could do it, not me. It wasn't a question of whether I could find someone to play with; it was the question of whether I can play at all. The other thing was, I thought that people could not hear me. You know how it is, you are trying to speak to an adult, and they are having a conversation with another adult, and when you have said something, they just don't react. It is as if you have spoken to a wall.

But either way, in one such party at some time in my life, I met my mother's sister. Sangeeta... I had never met her before because she lived in Dubai, and that was the first time in many years they had come here. It was an odd meeting. She had said

"How are you?"

And I had said "I am fine, aunty."

"Which standard are you in?"

"I am going to the fourth."

"You are a big boy now, and big people call other big people by name. You can call me Sangeeta."

"Really?"

"Why, is there a doubt?"

"I always thought since I was small, big people can't hear me."

"Really?"

"But you can hear me when I speak?"

"Loud and clear," she laughed.

At that time another adult came in and tried to cut our conversation. Now, if you were a kid growing up in India, you'd know that this is absolutely normal. A kid having a conversation with an adult is inconsequential. So anyone can cut it at any time. But when it happened this woman told the other adult.

"I am sorry. Let me complete this conversation with this young gentleman here, and I will be with you in a moment."

That was the first time I had been able to communicate with an adult. Uninterrupted. Can you imagine? The breakthrough I had had? An adult, a full-grown human being, a person who was able to hear other adults on a wavelength meant for adults, had been able to hear my voice. Not only that, she had smiled, acknowledged, asked questions, given me enough space to listen, and before all of that could get over, this adult, this mighty human being, had told another adult that her conversation with me mattered. I mattered.

That moment is of particular importance to me. As you can imagine, it was a moment of mighty decisions. An adult had given importance to a conversation involving me and my opinions. She had decided to ask the other adult to come back after some time. That decision came more spontaneously than I had thought. I had never imagined it could be that obvious for anyone, but it seems it was, and it seems it was the right thing to do.

From that day on, I used to look forward to conversations with her, and for some surprising reason, she looked forward to it too.

There never seemed to be a doubt in her mind to answer a phone call by me or think about picking up the phone and calling me herself. Inquiring about my progress, thinking about my future, you know all those kinds of things. But there was something extremely unique about her. She never thought my thoughts were stupid. There was a certain importance she gave me, my thoughts, my ideas and my abilities to speak.

You know we'd discuss all sorts of things. Politics, ideas, science, history. But not all of it was simple talk, you see. I wouldn't like losing debates, and if we had different opinions, I would argue, fight, look for evidence and even hold hour-long conversations. I would never back out, even if sometimes I knew I was wrong. But she, on the other hand, would never raise her voice but simply put her point forward. There were occasions when she acknowledged that she was wrong and categorically say 'I understand your point of view' or ' I agree to what you say' or simply 'You are right.'

As ten years went by, I realised that she had begun to trust my judgement. It felt good. I started to trust myself a bit more too, and soon, the other adults started to hear my voice. Not just heard, listened.

But there is one incident that defined my relationship with her. I remember it distinctly as if it happened yesterday. She was in town and dropped in one day and met me. Conversations began about thoughts, ideas and moved into some books she was reading, and out of nowhere, she asked me the question.

"Ravi, I have a problem. Will you help me decide?"

'Sure"

"I have a friend. She supports a small community in Mumbai, a community that has been suffering for ages. She needs some money and has asked for help. But to be able to, I will have to sell some jewellery. What should I do?"

What should she do? How would I know? I am not in her position, and she is an older person... Why didn't she take advice from someone who knows things? Someone who has the answers to such questions. Why had she come to me? Did she really expect me to answer that? She was the one who usually had all the answers. She read all those books and kept quoting from them.

"How would I know any of this?" I told her

"No one knows the answers to these questions. But they come to us all the time. The question is, how would you answer that question?"

"I might say something, and then you might have to do it."

"I will consider your opinion because yours matters."

"But I don't think I am qualified."

"No one is qualified."

"I don't even know the person you are talking about."

"I can introduce you to her if you'd like."

"And then I would have to take your decision?"

"You will only have to advise me, will you?"

"Yes."

I didn't go. There was something about the pressure of the situation I didn't like. Why was she making me do this? Maybe I disappointed her, maybe she would never speak to me again, maybe I had lost the only good friend I had managed to make, but that moment was scary. How could I decide what to do for a full-grown adult? You need to live for a certain number of years, and then you handle such things, don't you? At least, that was why I stopped answering her phone calls and avoided eye contact with her at the parties. There were a couple of episodes when I turned right around as soon as I saw her approaching me.

I did that many times until one day; she came right up to me...

"How are you?"

"I am alright. I hope your friend is doing fine. Did you... manage to... help her out?"

"I did."

"So you sold your jewellery to help a stranger?"

"Not a stranger. A friend."

"And was making that decision easy?"

"Not really. As you can see, many people in the family have chosen to not speak with me."

"I...I think... Maybe they are unhappy with you giving the money to someone who is not in the family."

"It's alright. I made a decision."

She was about to go when I said, "Sorry..."

"Why are you apologising?"

"I ran away from helping you make a decision."

"That's alright. I never expected you to make my decisions anyway. You see, we are people of privilege. We have the privilege of money, time, education, so this privilege clouds our vision. I always like to take advice from friends and people I trust so that I get to see a perspective that is not necessarily mine."

I mulled over that thought. She trusted me to make an important decision. It was good to know that someone can trust me. But didn't my running away abandon that trust? Was she right in trusting a loser like me in the first place?

I don't know.

I went through that position again and again. Reflected on that day repeatedly. Wondered. Imagined and tried to replay that decision everyday. It became an important moment that I still go over. I had three options, you see, three options. I could say yes and tell her she should give the money to her friend. That would be the morally right thing to do cause she had money; she lived in Dubai and had a steady source of income. She would, in the long run, be able to buy more jewellery, and even if she wouldn't, she could still lead a comfortable lifestyle without it.

On the other hand, there is this scenario where she says no to her friend. She decides not to give her anything because her responsibilities lie with her family. She needs to make sure her children get all the resources they saved up for and never let go of it.

But there is a third scenario, where she, like me, can decide not to answer at all. Let her friend not know what she's thinking of, and suspend all dialogue until she naturally forgets about it.

I tell you it is for certain that I have spent many hours of my life pondering about what to choose, and I am glad I never had to make that decision for her.

Time went by, and the years went by. I grew up, got an engineering degree and started working in a great job, got a wonderful life partner, and nothing went wrong until that day when the pandemic came knocking.

24 March 2020, the nation went into lockdown for 21 days

15 April, we went into one more for 19 days

4 May a third lockdown for 14 days

18 May another one for 14 days

Just like that, everything was shut. At that time, I only got to speak to Sangeeta and her husband Vivek through video calls. Our family in Dubai, like so many others in the world, kept living and working from home.

There were times when we spoke, there were times when we were quiet, and there were times when we were pretending nothing has happened and went about our business pounding away on keyboards as people died outside. But there was hope. They said India had very few cases compared to the other parts of the world, and the numbers were "steadily declining"

I called Dubai immediately, telling them that they could plan to come here since the cases were going down. It was my birthday. We could all celebrate together. I was happy to say that they were happy to hear it, and just like that, the unlocking began.

By the time December arrived, everything was open. Everything was available. People were out doing their businesses. Politicians were back to being political, and there was also an Indian Premier League. Things could not go wrong. Things would only improve now, wouldn't they?

That's when they bought their tickets. Tickets to Mumbai. Tickets to come and meet us. Tickets to discuss things and be social again. My family, who was distanced for over a year and a half, was coming, and it was time to celebrate.

February 2021, we had our first cup of coffee together. The conversation lasted for over four hours. She asked how I was feeling, and of course, when the kids wanted to speak to her, she gave them equal time and interest.

Life was good.

A vaccination programme against the dreaded virus had begun in India as well. We would be vaccinated. What could go wrong?

By Late- March, a second wave arrived.

On 5 April, the country reported its largest single-day increase in cases, just over 103,000.

It would be fine, I told myself.

On 9 April, India surpassed 1 million active cases.

On 12 April, India overtook Brazil in active covid numbers.

It would be fine, I told myself.

On 15th April, the virus entered our homes.

It would be fine I told myself.

A total of five members of our family got the virus.

One among them was Sangeeta, the other her husband, Vivek. The other three were my wife, my child and my sister.

It would be fine, I told myself.

I could not see them as they isolated in their rooms.

I tried to distract myself by watching television.

It would be fine, I told myself.

On television, I saw religious ceremonies, political rallies, millions of people assembled, the Indian premier league, cricketers in advertisements, actors selling broadband internet, news of oxygen shortage, patients gasping for breath, angry citizens fighting with helpless doctors, crematoriums, and bodies upon bodies mounting.

It would be fine, I told myself.

At around midnight, Vivek and Sangeeta's oxygen saturation levels fell.

97

95

90

88

85

I could not enter the room. Their voices came from within. They needed to breathe.

I called. The phones rang. Hospitals full. Ambulances unavailable. Doctors desperate. War rooms silent. God Dead...

I wore my mask, knocked on the door and said.

"I need to take you to the hospital. Now."

"What about the kids and..." they choked.

"They are asymptomatic. You need to come. Now"

They gathered themselves as I took them to the car. I remember the drive. It took a long time to reach the hospital even though there was no one on the streets. We reached the hospital.

"Can I take them to the emergency"

"We don't have beds."

"I just want some..."

"No beds available."

I turned the car around and took them to the next hospital.

"Excuse me"

"No Beds available."

Next hospital

"Excuse Me"

"No beds"

Next Hospital

"Ex…"

"No Beds…"

As we went from hospital to hospital we realised that there was a possibility that there were no beds available in the whole city. That is precisely when the phone rang…

"We've found one bed. Come quickly"

It was mom. She had been calling every hospital in town when we were away. When we reached the hospital, I realised the most important question… One bed? We had two patients. How would one bed suffice?

That's when Vivek told me.

"Let her take the bed."

"But..."

"No buts... It is because of me she is in this condition."

"No, it is ..."

"Listen. Let her take this bed, and tell her that I will get one too."

"How can I..."

"This is my decision. Not yours."

I looked at him. How had he made that decision so easily? One bed? One life? How did he come to the conclusion? Sangeeta kept looking at him as she was wheeled away into the one and only bed that the city could offer.

It didn't take long before Vivek was gone. Perhaps he was gone the moment she left. The last parting glance they had among each other was the final moment of his life. I don't think I remember much after that.

I do remember the chaos. More news anchors on large plasma screen televisions in the hospital. Political rallies. Speeches. The people screaming. New patients arriving. Among them a young man and his young wife. She was weeping, and he was breathless.

The sounds of gasping.

More gasping.

It is etched in my memory.

As time refused to go by, I stood at the precipice of this day and looked into the night, thinking about how my first friend was gasping for air. Trying to breathe the little she could breathe. How could I help her? How should I help her? I looked around for answers. The lady who had arrived with her husband was near me. She was looking for the same answers perhaps. What could she do? What should she do?

"We're running out of oxygen. Only six hours left."

The doctor was petrified, fear dripping from the forehead.

"We are trying to arrange."

We both stared at each other for a while. What was I supposed to do? A daze hit me. The day was not over. Vivek was gone. Sangeeta was hardly able to breathe. I hadn't told anyone about it, and now the oxygen was running out. I was tired. Broken. Needed to sleep. Needed to grieve. But there was no time. I would lose both of them if I don't go. I saw the woman running; perhaps I needed to run too. I ran.

That night I looked everywhere. Chemists. Distributors. I called government helplines. Spoke to the authorities. But it was not until 4 am that I found one cylinder of Oxygen.

When I found it, I finally could breathe a little easier myself. You know, this disease is funny, it chokes you whether you have it or not.

I looked at it. What was it in this cylinder that held everyone hostage? Can this save her?

I looked at the nurse, who was frantically making phone calls. But at that moment, the woman who had her husband admitted walked in.

"I could not find Oxygen anywhere. No one has it. Can you help me? Does anyone have it? Can anyone help me with a little …Oxygen?"

I had Oxygen. But it was meant to save Sangeeta's life. Why couldn't she find one for herself?

My eyes land on the newspapers nearby.
Pharmacist held for black marketing of oxygen regulator

Police raids hoarders of medical oxygen

HC appeals to citizens not to hoard oxygen cylinders

Perhaps that's why.

It seemed everyone wanted it. It all came to this moment. This, very important moment in my life. I looked at the cylinder and then to the desperation of this woman who must have been twenty-five years old. Her husband inside, gasping for breath.

My eyes glance at the calendar. The date strikes me. Today is Sangeeta's birthday. What are the odds?

I had two options before me. Either I could take the cylinder to save Sangeeta. It seems the most obvious thing to do for me.

Either I could give it to this woman, who so desperately needed it. Something which I cannot do right now. But what should I do, walk past her? There is nothing wrong in doing that, is there? She is a stranger. I don't know her. I should try to save my own first. If that's the truth, why can't I look this stranger in the face? That face covered with a mask tells me that she, too, has a story. Perhaps they married recently. Maybe they were back from their honeymoon. The eyes that look at me are screaming for help, and I know one thing, that even though I don't know it, her relationship with her husband is important. It matters. It's her Oxygen. Why are decisions so difficult?

Now whether this cylinder is good enough to save people's lives, I don't know. I also don't know if one cylinder is enough or if we need more. All I know is this was the most important thing for me right now.

What would Sangeeta do?

She'd ask...

I think I can do with some advice too. What would you do?

(Addresses the audience)

What would you do if you were in my position?

(Goes to the member of the audience and hands over the cylinder of Oxygen to him/her)

Don't worry, you are not really in my position, but I would really like to know.

You can either give it to Sangeeta.

or you can give it to the lady over there...

or you have a third choice, and this could be your decision too. You could decide not to do anything because you really are not in my position.

(Allow the audience member to make that choice. Whatever the choice is, respect it)

HIMALI KOTHARI

After trudging along the beaten path for a few years, Himali Kothari veered off in search of a more fulfilling journey. Some soul-searching combined with karmic coincidences led her to reacquaint with her childhood hobby of writing and in 2007, she took her first tentative step as a writing professional. Since then, she has written on travel, design, food, lifestyle, books and general interest topics for print magazines and online portals.

Somewhere along the way, Himali discovered her knack for shaping raw manuscripts into stories and donned the hat of creative editor for stories-in-progress. In 2011, she launched a writing workshop at Xavier's Institute of Communication, which has been attended by novice and experienced writers seeking to hone their skills. She also conducts bespoke workshops for educational and corporate organizations.

As Scriptwriter and Creative Editor at Readings in the Shed, Himali is involved in writing original scripts and adapting available stories and events into scripts for performance.

Coming
of Age

Pushpa opened her mouth wide and tried to push the cough out. It felt like it was wedged between her lungs and her throat. She curved her spine into a C, rubbed her chest and scratched at her throat. Something would dislodge it. It was a few seconds before relief came. The sound filled the room, her ears, her head. It went on for a few minutes. Her mouth was covered with the end of her sari, but when she pulled it away, it was dry. She propped her head up against the wall, pressed her palm on her chest, and rubbed it as hard as she could. And coughed again. More sound. Just sound. She dropped her head back into the mattress and closed her eyes.

"Dadiji, do you need more water?" Meera had opened the door of the room just enough to pop her head in.

Pushpa shook her head and pointed at the pot next to her mattress. Her mattress had been moved here three days ago when the cough started. It was Meera and Rakesh's room. Earlier it had been Pushpa's son's and daughter-in-law's room. Pushpa had always slept on a mattress in a corner in the front room. After her son died, her daughter-in-law had moved into another corner in the room. And later, as Rakya and Meera's daughter grew older, she moved in there too.

Pushpa's eyes filled up at the thought of her great-granddaughter. Every night Soni would roll out both their mattresses side-by-side, lie down on her stomach and look up at Pushpa. At times Pushpa would mock shut her eyes and pretend to be asleep.

Soni's little finger would poke her side, "Badidadi? Badidadi? Are you sleeping?"

Pushpa would open one eye, "One eye is asleep. One eye is awake." And she would waggle her eyebrow as if trying to push open the other one forcibly. It always made the child burst into giggles.

"Story, badidadi," and Soni would throw her little arm across Pushpa and lay her head on her chest and wait for her to start. Those ten minutes were what got Pushpa through the day. But their story sessions had come to a stop three nights ago after Pushpa moved into the room. All she had seen of Soni in these three days was when she opened the door a crack and pushed her head in for a few seconds. That was all she had seen of anyone. A plate with her meals would be placed at the door, and the emptied plate collected back from the same spot. Meera had come in once to put a pot of water in the room. Pushpa told her she was feeling fine, and it was just a minor cough.

"Should I make gud-roti for Soni when she comes home from school?"

"Dadiji, for a few days, don't cook. Rest in the room. And when you go to the lavatory, cover your mouth with a cloth."

"Why? What is wrong? Have I got TB?"

"No, dadiji, it's not TB. You will be fine in a few days, but it is better if you stay in the room till then. And tell me if you want anything."

Pushpa nodded and lay down on the mattress. She had not told Meera that her joints had been aching for the past two nights. She had not thought much of it. *When you live long enough to see your fourth-generation, bones ache.*

"All night, she was coughing. I barely got any sleep." Pushpa heard her daughter-in-law's voice through the door. Soni had left it ajar when she had peeked in after she returned from school.

"She was also warm to the touch. I am worried, Ma. It has been five days."

"You touched her?"

"Yes. When I took food to her."

"You should have left the food near the door. Rakya said we are not to go near her."

"I had covered my face, Ma. And she also covered her mouth with her sari. I was care-"

"Don't argue with me. What if she has that virus that Rakya was telling us about?"

"Ma, we can't just leave her in that room. Her cough has become worse in the last two days."

"It is probably because of the change in weather."

"Also, body ache. She doesn't say it but-"

"At her age, of course, her body will ache."

"She has not complained about it before. Earlier, she had no trouble sitting at the chullah or sitting on the floor. But, yesterday, she struggled to sit up on the mattress. I think I should go to the clinic and speak to the doctor."

"No. No. Let's wait. If the neighbours catch a scent of it, we will not be able to step out. Sarita's husband has been coughing for years from all the tobacco. But, ever since this new disease has come up, no one goes anywhere near them. Doctor sahib said he does not have the virus, but what if he is wrong?"

"He's a doctor Ma; he knows what he's-"

"He is not God, no? You keep quiet. What if Rakya is not allowed to work at the construction site? What will we do? And, don't you dare bother him with all your nonsense."

"But Ma, if it is the virus and we don't do something, we all could fall sick. It could spread to more people in the village. The people from the Nagar Palika came and put posters everywhere - Don't hide, get treatment."

"The Nagar Palika has nothing to do except put up posters about something or the other."

"Soni's teacher also spoke about it to them. It is everywhere - Bambai, Delhi, the whole world. I don't think we should hide it. You and Rakesh-"

"You and your daughter are the only sensible people in this house. I am dumb. Rakya is dumb. But you two, you'll know it all."

"Ma, all I am saying is that it is too much of a risk for Dadiji. She is too old."

"Then, maybe God has decided it is her time."

"Ma!"

"Oh-ho. What? It's not like she can hear me. She has been half-deaf for years now."

Pushpa turned her face to the wall. It was true. She was too old. But she wasn't deaf. Some years ago, her daughter-in-law assumed she was going deaf, and Pushpa decided not to correct her. There was not much that anyone wanted to say to her, and there was not much that she wanted to hear. Meera had suggested going to the village clinic and asking about some machine for the ear, but thankfully Rakya and his mother had shushed her.

"What is so important that she need to hear at her age?"

"She can spend the rest of her days in peace."

This countdown to her last days did not bother Pushpa. From the time she could remember, her life had been on a countdown. From before she was born.

"I was waiting for those nine months to get over. I knew everything would change once I had my baby in my arms," her mother would tell her. "Your belly is low, everyone told me, it will be a boy." And then she would look at Pushpa and slowly nod her head, her eyes filled with tears for that boy who did not come. Every few months, a spark would replace those tears.

"Your little brother is going to come in a few months," she would tell Pushpa.

Pushpa loved those few weeks. Her mother would cuddle her and kiss her, and they would think of names for her little brother. But he never came. It always ended in a pool of blood soaking her mother's sari. With every passing year, Pushpa saw her mother sink further into her own body until one day she turned invisible.

So silly. How did it help not to be seen? They knew you were there. Their feet tamped down harder on you. The barbs were sharper, louder. It was so much better to turn blind.

And, that's what Pushpa did after her mother turned invisible. She stopped seeing. She did not see chhoti maa who baba brought home. She did not see the laddoos that were distributed when her stepbrother was born. She did not see the marigolds strung all over the house once a year. She did not see the halwa cooked on that day, though the aroma of the ghee and sugar floated through the house and snaked into her nostrils. It was her brother's birthday, she learnt. *Birth-day. The day he was born? What was so special about that? Why did they make such a fuss? Everyone is born.*

"I was too," she had told him one day.

"Oh ya?" he had asked. "When?"

"It's a secret."

"You don't know. You don't know," he had chanted.

"How old are you, amma?"

Pushpa opened her eyes but shut them again. The light made her head throb.

"Is your head hurting?" the voice said.

Pushpa opened her eyes into narrow slits. A vision in white glowed by her mattress. She was covered head-to-toe in white. All Pushpa could see were the eyes. They were smiling. Pushpa took a deep breath. *Had her time finally come? Was this angel there to take her away? She was ready.* She started to sit up on the mattress.

"No, no," the angel said. "You need to rest. Lie down." She stretched her hand out and stroked her head. "I'll come back soon."

Tears filled Pushpa's eyes as the angel walked away.

"Isn't it time to marry her off?"

Baba grunted in reply to chhoti maa.

"She has been getting the monthly curse for a year now. It is risky to keep her in the house. What if she goes and does something? It will become a nuisance. Find a match for her and be done with it."

A few days later, Pushpa was summoned to baba's room.

"Your wedding date is fixed for three weeks from today. Pack the things you have to take with you," baba said as he turned the page of the newspaper.

"How many clothes? For how many days are you sending me away?" Pushpa had mumbled.

Baba had looked up from the newspaper and furrowed his eyebrows. *It's me, Pushpa,* she wanted to say. *He hadn't seen her since... Had*

he seen her ever? Maybe he didn't recognize her.
She stared back but then remembered she was
blind and dropped her eyes.

"How many days? Forever, stupid girl," chhoti
maa had said.

And then the countdown to her marriage began.

"Listen to what he says. And obey him and his
mother. Don't argue with anyone. If they send
you back, you watch it," chhoti maa chanted at
Pushpa every chance she got.

These instructions did not worry Pushpa. This
was what her mother had instructed her to do
since she was a toddler. It was how she had
lived the first thirteen years of her life. *How was
marriage any different? Why did everyone make
such a big deal about it?*

"It won't be anything like here," chhoti ma added.
"Maybe then you will appreciate the comforts you
have enjoyed in your father's house."

When the day came, Pushpa saw the marigolds
strung around the house. She saw *halwa* being
stirred in a huge cauldron in the courtyard. She
saw the red sari that they draped around her and
pulled over her eyes. And when she peeked up
from under it, she saw her husband. He towered

over her and had a thick curly moustache. Like baba. Pushpa shuddered and began to shut her eyes. But, she swallowed her breath, glanced up again and lifted her eyes till they met his. They were smiling. Like baba's did every year on her brother's birthday. The day after the wedding, Pushpa was bundled into a bullock cart with her belongings, her husband and his family and sent off.

For the first few days, this new house seemed to be just like her father's house. Pushpa had chores to do just like she had done at home. Sweep and cook and clean. And, if she made a mistake, her mother-in-law would slap her, like chhoti maa had, or give her only a little rice for lunch.

But, in the evening, when her husband came home, the house would change. His eyes would smile at her when she offered him water. After they had eaten the evening meal, her mother-in-law and dadi would go and lay down in the adjacent room. Her husband would pick out a book from the almirah and sit in the kitchen with his back against the wall. Pushpa watched him as she washed the dinner vessels and cleaned the kitchen. *What was inside those pages?* She could see his eyes flitter back and forth, back and forth. And, he would barely look up, even when a vessel clanged to the floor.

The first few days, Pushpa was too scared to go anywhere near him. But soon, curiosity got the better of her. *What was hiding in those pages? Jesters*, she decided, when she heard him burst into laughter one day. But, the next day, his eyes looked moist and his jaw tight. So, she would sweep close to where he sat and tried to get a peek. And then, one day, he looked up just as she was trying to steal a glance.

"Do you want to listen to a story?" he asked and patted a spot across from him.

From that day, every night after she finished the housework, she would sit in that same spot and wait for a new story. Every day, he would tell her about the people and places in his books. Pushpa would sit in that spot; her eyes stuck on him till he closed the book shut. And then she would go into the room where her mother-in-law and dadi slept while he rolled out his mattress in that same spot where he read.

"Why can't I sleep next to you?" she had asked him one day after he shut the book close.

"You will. When you are old enough."

"How old is enough?"

He had laughed at that, his eyes, his moustache and his torso, "How old are you now?"

Pushpa stared back at him, panic filling her throat. She didn't know. Nobody knew. She had asked every year on her stepbrother's birthday but they shooed her off. *How would she know when she was old enough? She would never be able to sleep next to him.* Tears ran down her cheeks.

"Don't worry," he said, patting her head. "I will write to your father and ask him."

More tears spilt out. *Baba would not know. If he did, he would have decorated the house with flowers and ordered chhoti maa to make halwa. Nobody knew.*

"Leave it to me," he said. "I'll find out."

Many weeks went past. The stories continued, but there was no mention of her age. Pushpa was not surprised; she knew baba would have been of no help. And then one night, when she sat down in her spot, he closed the book he had been reading from and took out a piece of paper from his kurta pocket.

"I know how old you are," he said and tapped his forefinger on the paper. "It is written inside this."

He unfolded the paper and laid it in her hands. Pushpa stroked the black creatures that crawled on it and looked up at him.

"Put this paper in that trunk you brought from your father's house and make sure you keep it safe."

Pushpa looked at the machine on her index finger. It was blinking with lights. The white angel had come back.

"She is doing very well," the angel told Meera, who was squatting next to her by Pushpa's mattress. "This virus is usually cruel to the old."

Pushpa looked at the angel. *Why was she talking to Meera? Hadn't she come for her?*

"Ma, doctor madam, says dadiji will be okay," Meera shouted out towards the door.

The angel added, "She's past the contagious period. You all can come in and sit with her. She'll like it, after so many days of being alone."

The angel took the machine off her finger, Oxygen levels are stable. Amma, you are made of solid stuff. You might be the oldest survivor in the country." She turned to Meera, "Do you know how old she is? Do you'll have a birth certificate or a document or something?"

Meera shook her head, "I don't think so, but I will check in the almirahs."

"Yes, let me know if you find something. She must be close to hundred years, I guess. I am sure the government would like to honour her if she is the oldest survivor."

"Doctor madam said the government might honour dadiji as the oldest survivor. Do we have any proof of her age?"

"Honour her with what? Cash prize?"

"I don't know. She said to look for a document with her birth date."

"I don't remember seeing any such document. Search the house. If anything is there, it will be somewhere."

"Okay."

"Some money would be good. As it is, I've lost out on two weeks of wages. Serve me some more rice."

Pushpa turned towards the wall and closed her eyes. Over the next few days, every drawer, box, cupboard in the house was turned inside out.

"Did you check properly? Maybe it is somewhere in between her sarees."

"She has five sarees, Ma. If it were there, we would have found it."

"And the old woman is of no help at all. I sat for hours with her yesterday and asked her if she remembered any paper. Not a word from her. I know she could hear me, but nothing. Not even a nod of her head. She just closed her eyes."

"She must be tired. Doctor madam said she needs rest."

"Stop with your doctor, madam said this, doctor madam said that. What has she been doing all these days except resting? She is just being difficult."

That night Pushpa told Soni the story of the man who gave her, her birth date. She stroked her head as the child fell asleep with her head in the crook of her neck. Pushpa lay awake as the moon rose in the sky. She lay awake till her daughter-in-law's rumbling snores calmed to whispers.

The full moon cast a dim light, enough for Pushpa to make her way to the narrow space between the rear of the house and the boundary wall. The corner was piled with discarded things. The in-between things. Not thrown. Nor kept in the house. Some broken pots. Rakya's old toys. His father's walking stick. Some slabs of stone left over from when the lavatory was built. A half-empty can of paint. Pushpa picked her way through it to the corner. There it was, behind the corroded aluminium sheet that had covered the hole in the roof before it was repaired. The trunk from baba's house.

Pushpa pulled it out of the heap and sat down with her back against the house wall. It opened without any difficulty; the locks had long crumbled to dust. Her wedding sari was in it. The zari border had turned black, and the fabric was fraying in some places. It had been red like the bindi that had been painted on her head that day. Now, it was the colour of the rust-hued sand that the wind blew in and scattered across the house. She lifted it up. Glass bangles fell out and into the trunk. Pushpa slipped the bangles on her wrists and draped the sari around her.

The paper was at the bottom of the trunk. Safe. All these years, she had never taken it out. The creases at the folds tore when she unfolded it. She laid it out on her knee and stroked the creatures that crawled over it. They, too, had wrinkled and greyed.

Pushpa sat there, her back against the wall clutching the paper in her fist. The moonlight had turned brighter and more stars had turned up. The temperature had dropped, and a cool breeze had pushed its way into this forgotten space. Pushpa pulled her wedding sari tighter around her. She felt a caress on her forehead and looked up. It was a white angel with smiling eyes.

They found her the next day. The open trunk by her side. Bangles on her wrist glinting in the sun and her wedding sari around her. When they laid her down and pried her fist open, sawdust fell out and crawling amidst it were some grey-black creatures. Nobody could figure out what they were. No one had seen them before.

The Birthday Stories

"Whose birthday is it today?" the yellow-black striped snake with googly eyes yelled out.

I scanned the group seated cross-legged in a cluster that had settled on the floor around. They gaped back at the snake on the platform in front of us. It was an easy answer, but no one spoke. I obviously could not answer. How obnoxious would it be for the birthday girl herself to speak up?

My older cousins at the fringe of the cluster ignored the question and continued to chat. Some of my friends and classmates had mumbled my name under their breaths. But it had not been a coordinated chorus, so it had sounded like a bundle of spat out, incoherent sounds. Undeterred by this unenthusiastic response, the snake continued at his articulate best.

"I can't hear you," he admonished. "Whose birthday is it today?"

"Ritu's," one voice rang out, from closer to the fringe of the circle.

I looked over in the direction of the voice. Aakarsh. He threw me a toothy smile. I responded with a toothless stretch of my lips. He was wearing a grey waistcoat over an electric blue shirt and grey pants. Who wore a waistcoat to a birthday party?

"That's correct!" replied the snake. "And how old is she today?" He sounded relieved to have found an ally in the audience.

"Ten," Aakarsh yelled out.

"Very good," said the snake and his googly eyes danced manically.

Big deal. Everyone knew the answer. But, Aakarsh had to speak over everyone else because he was, well him! Always the first to raise his hand in class as well. Nerd. So annoying. If only mom had listened to me when she was put his name on the guest list.

"But, mom, Aakarsh is not even my friend."

"Don't be silly. Of course, he is. The two of you got along so well when we all went to Goa together."

"That was ages ago, mom. I don't like him now."

"Why? He is such a nice boy. Polite. And so obedient and caring towards his mother. You could learn from him."

"Oh, please. He is a weirdo. Everyone at school thinks so. Nobody even talks to him."

"That's enough, Ritu. I have put his name down."

"It is my party, not yours."

But, mom had moved on to the next item on her checklist. And, so there he was, shouting out responses at the snake as if they were best chums. Showoff.

"Happy birthday, Ritu," Aakarsh came up to me after the puppet show. He held out a glossy paper bag that had balloons, clowns and Happy Birthday printed on it.

"Thanks." I took the bag from his hands.

"It is the complete set of Malory Towers. Enid Blyton's your favourite author, right? Mine too."

"Whoa! This is amazing. I have been dying to read these. How did you get them? I got the first one at the book store, but they said the rest of the series is not available yet."

"Papa got them from London. I have read the first one as well, and I loved it."

"Oh. You didn't want to keep them for yourselves?"

"Mumma and I thought it would be the best gift for you."

Thank God, mom wasn't around. She would have lectured me then and there about what a good boy Aakarsh was and how I could be more like him. Okay, the incredible gift apart, who refers to their mother as 'Mumma'? What was he, two? Book six shimmered at me again, and I could see Darrell on the cover page shaking her disappointed head at me. Okay, okay. I was going to be nice. For Enid.

"You can borrow these after I finish reading them if you like."

"Really?" He flashed that big smile again. "That would be awesome."

*****

Two metallic balloons, 1 and 6, bobbed in the corner of the room. The helium made their heads boop the ceiling, and their strings kept them tethered to the table. More silver and black balloons floated along the floor. As promised, my parents had left, half an hour into the party. The neon lights on the ceiling had kicked into action, and the DJ had started with the latest dance tracks. Most of us had not moved off the dance floor for the last two hours. I glanced towards the door as my friends synced their moves to the Macarena. Where was he? Was he seriously going to ditch me on my birthday? It was not a possibility I had ruled out. It had been tough to get him to agree to come.

"What do you mean - do I have to come?" I had hissed at Aakarsh as he read the invite.

"I mean, you will be stuck with your giggling gaggle. What will I do?"

"Stop calling them that. And I am inviting the whole class. Our class, Aakarsh. Stop acting like they are strangers."

"But, they are. Barely anyone in class speaks to me. Not that I-"

"That's because of that permanent expression on your face."

"What expression?"

"The   you-are-too-stupid-to-deserve-my-valuable-time-so-stay-away expression."

"That's crap. I have tried to talk to them, but they are super boring. And when they are not boring, they are crass. Which, by the way, they consider hilarious."

"See? There it is. The I-am-better-than-everyone-"

"So you are on their side now?"

"Of course, I am not on their side. All I am saying is that you have to be at my party."

"Ya ya. I will be there. How else will I give you your gift?"

The hour hand on my wristwatch was inching towards twelve, but no Aakarsh yet. So, this is what Cinderella must have felt like. Then, one minute before twelve, the door swung open, and he stepped in as if he had been waiting all this while to make a dramatic entrance. I waited to catch his eyes so that he would see my nostrils flare and then turned away. A table with my birthday cake had been rolled to the centre of the room. After the birthday song and the ceremonial cake feeding, everyone drifted off towards the buffet.

"Happy birthday," Aakarsh held out the gift-wrapped package to me.

"Glad you could make it," I kept my arms folded across my chest and gave him the most apparent fake smile I could conjure.

"I am here, no? Now, will you please take this? I have been waiting to give this to you."

There are times when you have to squash your ego, even if it bites into your heels. This was one of those times. I grabbed my gift from his hand and peeled away the cello tape. Aakarsh was shifting his weight from one foot to the other. When he first gave me Malory Towers on my tenth birthday, neither of us imagined it would become a tradition. On my eleventh, it was Daddy Long Legs and the year after Charlie and the Chocolate Factory. Last year it was Pride and Prejudice, and it hooked me on a steady dose of old-fashioned English romances. When I wasn't reading them, I was fantasizing about being wooed by Mr Darcy.

Once one side of the package was open, the book slid out, The Writing Life by Annie Dillard. My heart plummeted to the dance floor. Why had he been so excited to give this one to me? For the last six years, he had picked the perfect book for me. He was not as much of a reader now as he had been, but somehow he knew what I would want to read. And he had never disappointed. Until today. A textbook on writing? I flipped the book over to the blurb - *In these short essays…dedication, absurdity, and daring… experiences while writing…insight into one of the most mysterious professions.* I looked up at him, eyebrows raised. What was he getting at?

He snatched the book away from my hand and read on, "For writers, it is a warm, rambling conversation with a stimulating and extraordinarily talented colleague."

"Aakarsh, if this gift is a code for something, I will need a hammer to crack it."

"Three months ago, you told me that maybe you would like to be a writer. Don't you remember?"

"I wasn't serious. I don't have a clue on how to become a writer."

"That's why this book," and he tapped his index finger on the quote that he had read out to me.

"Aakarsh, I was fantasizing, as I do about going to England and bumping into Darcy. I mean, how do I even know if I am any good at writing?"

"Of course you are. Your essays are the best in school. And you have always been the favourite of all our English teachers right from grade one."

"That does not-"

"Don't diss the idea, Rits. Read the book."

"Writing is not a DIY manual. You read a book, and voila, you are a writer."

"Look, let's not discuss this now. Your giggling gaggle is missing you," he pointed at my friends seated at a table with plates of food.

"And you? You are going to flee now that you have given me my gift, aren't you?"

"No. I'll go and hang out with the boys. I have been practising some new expressions I want to try out on them."

*****

I slid onto the high bar stool that Aakarsh was holding in place. He was always so chivalrous, straight out of the Mills and Boons I had devoured by the kilos. Okay, some of the guys in my Master's class were not bad either - pulling out chairs, offering to bring coffee from the self-service counter, holding jackets. It was just unusual to see it in an Indian guy. And with Aakarsh, it wasn't in the UK that had brought it out. He had always been like that.

"Lucky we found a table. I've never managed one on Friday night. We just hang out at the bar," he pointed to the long glass table that stretched along the length of one wall. The word 'Baracoa', each letter twisted out of flattened metal strips, was nailed to the bare brick wall behind it. Bottles of whiskey, vodka, wine and other spirits that I did not have a clue about were stacked on the wooden shelf under the letters. Overhead, lights bathed everything in a purple glow - the wall, the bottles, the bar table and the faces crowding the table.

"Hey, birthday girl," Aakarsh tapped my palm with his index finger. "What are you drinking?"

I opened my mouth, but before I could speak, he held up his forefinger, "Do not say club soda with lime juice. You are not turning twenty-one with a soft drink. At least get a cocktail?"

"Okay. A mojito."

"Whoa, someone did not need convincing. And I was all ready with my speech on the merits of getting drunk. Are you a closet alcoholic, Rits?" he placed both his hands on his cheeks and dropped his jaw in mock surprise before heading off towards the glowing bar.

It was close to midnight, and the club was thronging with dancing bodies. The bodies on the dance floor swayed and gyrated to whatever the speaker was spewing. I cocked my ear towards the speakers, but if there was a song bleating out from them, it was lost on me. But then, my recall of what I broadly classified as 'English songs' did not go beyond the first five of the MTV Top 20.

This was my fourth night out in the one and a half semester that we had been in Leeds. Shameful, given the city's throbbing club scene. Aakarsh, though, had been out every Friday and Saturday from the very first week. It had shocked me initially. He hadn't been that much of a party person when we were in Bombay. And I had no clue how he had made friends that quick. Back home, I had pretty much been his only friend. He'd asked me to go along a few times at the start of term but then gave up. The one time I did go, something had been off. It seemed like he did not know how to hang out with me. Odd, considering we were together all the time in Bombay. So much so that I was constantly fielding the 'Is there something going on?' question from my friends. But, that night had been strange, uncomfortable.

So, we settled into a routine. After the last lecture on Friday, I'd bid him goodbye for the weekend. And on Sunday afternoon, my phone would beep - Dinner? Yours, mine or out? Until today.

"We are here only for a year, Rits. And it's your twenty-first. Let's do your birthday the Leeds way," he had insisted. I agreed.

Aakarsh was manoeuvring back through the crowd, the glasses held above his head. Halfway back, he stopped at a group on the fringe of the dance floor. None of the faces in the group was familiar to me. They were not from Uni. But, Aakarsh knew them, and from their animated expressions, it was clear that they were thrilled to see him. They gestured to him to stay, but he shook his head and nodded in my direction. Only after he had hugged and kissed each one of them that he continued towards our table. Who were these people? And since when had Aakarsh become a serial hugger and kisser? I was his best friend, and the only time I could remember him hugging me was when I was upset.

"Here you go, senorita. Your mojito." He placed the drinks on the table, scooted his high chair next to mine and sat down on it.

"Somebody is very popular," I raised an eyebrow at him.

"Them? Just the weekend clubbing gang."

"They don't look familiar. I thought you partied with the peeps from the MBA class."

"Initially. But then I met these people, and they are more fun so…»

"They like you, it seems. We can hang out with them if you want. I don't mind."

"Nah. Tonight's about you." He placed one arm around my shoulders and gave me a side-hug. More hugging? What was going on?

"Oh-kay. What is going on with-"

"Where were you at lunch today? You just messaged - busy."

"Meeting with the group for the project for Marketing Strategy class."

"Oh. Are you beginning to warm up to it?"

"Not really. But you gotta do what you gotta do, right?"

"I still don't understand whatever possessed you to take up a Masters in Marketing."

"Oh god, Aks. Don't start with me."

"You should have gone for that writing course at the New School in New York."

"And what would I have done after that course? I don't have a frigging clue. At least after this one,

I will have options. And I can always write on the side while I work."

He shook his head, "I don't know why you won't take yourself seriously as a writer."

"You are the only one who thinks I could be a writer. No one else-"

"I don't want to argue with you on your birthday, so let's drop it. For now."

"Thank you, much obliged. And by the way, if I was in NY, how would we have kept up our tradition of bringing in my birthday?"

"Touche, mademoiselle." He looked at his watch, "Speaking of which, it is almost time." He raised his glass and clinked it with mine, "Happy birthday Rits. Here's to many more midnight wishes."

"Thank you et al. Now, give me my gift," I reached out for the package he had placed on the table.

He clutched my palm before I could pull my gift away, "Rits, please don't open it right now. Open it later, in your flat."

"But, I always open my gift with you. It's our thing."

"I know. Just this once. Please."

I wanted to protest. But, there was something in the way he was clinging on to my hand that stopped me.

"Okay," I said and slipped it into my purse. "So, Mr Popular, are you going to show me your kind of a Friday night or are we only going to sit here?"

It was close to dawn when I got to my flat, and my eyelids struggled to stay open. But, there was no way I would go one more minute without opening Aakarsh's gift. It had been on my mind all night, and it had been tempting to sneak away into the loo and uncover the book. But, something told me it would upset him, and so I desisted. A few times that night, I had caught him looking at me as if he was trying to figure something out. When I would raise my eyebrows in response, he would start to open his mouth to speak, then clam it shut and nod his head. Bizarre.

I kicked off my heels, jumped on the bed and ripped open the glittering wrapping paper. It was a book like it had been every year since my tenth birthday. Why had he behaved so odd about a book? I turned it over - A Boy's Own Story by Edmund White. I turned to the blurb and scanned it - *In this, the first...coming-of-age during the 1950s...gay life in American fiction. Ridiculed by...solace in literature...sense of shame... struggle to accept.*

I stopped and reread it slowly. And then one more time. With every word, the fog that had descended on me through that evening began to lift. His friends at the bar. His panic when he gave me the book. The way he had squeezed my hand when I told him bye in the taxi. It all made sense now.

I could picture him in his flat waiting for a call or a message from me. He would have known I would unwrap it the moment I got into my flat. He would know the very moment I would have figured it out. But, what was I going to say to him? I did not have experience in dealing with this whole coming out thing. This was a first for me. I had only associated the h-word with celebrities, not regular people. Hell, I had just about begun to understand what it meant. What was the right thing to say? Had I seen an Oprah episode about this? I started to type a message to him and deleted it. I typed and deleted. Typed. Deleted.

And then, between the repeated taps on the backspace key, it dawned on me. I was not shocked. This was not some grand revelation like he had thought it was going to be. I had always known. Without knowing.

And then I knew what I needed to say. What I wanted to say.

"I love you, Aks, and I always will."

*****

I ran the brush through my hair one more time, darkened the kohl on the lower lid, checked myself in the mirror and settled down in front of the laptop. A click on 'Join with Video' brought my face up on the 14-inch screen. Oh no, that would not do. My usual double chin had turned into three from that angle. I placed a stack of books under the laptop. There, that was much better.

The phone beeped. It was Aakarsh - Sorry, hon, just got home. Logging on in 5.

Cool, I wrote back.

A glass of Cointreau, on the rocks, and a slice of tiramisu were by the laptop. I pictured Aakarsh rushing about his apartment. He would pour out a glass of his favourite red, bring it to the dining table and switch on his laptop.

Two minutes later, a second rectangle popped up on my screen, "Hello hello hello birthday girl."

"Haha. Hardly girl. I am forty. Yikes, Aks. I am forty."

"Bah! Age is just a number."

"Ya ya. You are only saying that because you have been that number for some three months already."

"Come on. We look good for a couple of forty-year-olds."

"Speak for yourself. I look like a dumpy old auntie."

"Stop bashing yourself. You look amazing."

"You are the only one who thinks that. I should chat with you more often. You are good for my ego."

"You need to get out. Or better yet, get on an app. And, then write a memoir about your love life."

"If the theme is my love life, then it will most definitely be fiction, not a memoir."

"At least that will get you writing. Last time you told me you would set aside a couple of hours every day to write. How's that going?"

"Cannot manage with work. I am so exhausted by the end of the day. All I want to do is binge on junk food and junk shows. There's no time right now. In a couple of years, hopefully, I can ease off on work and focus on the writing."

"Make the time, Rits, don't wait for it. You don't know what's around the corner."

His eyes flickered away from the screen, and I could see his Adam's apple wobble from the empty gulp before he turned his eyes back to me. I could see that he was holding on to that smile, straining to make sure it would not slip.

"Aks, how are you? Really."

I knew he was going to shrug, wave his hand and say he was doing fine. That he was busy with work but also hanging out with friends. All the right words. All the words he thought I needed to hear.

"Aks, it's me. You don't need to put on an act."

He was quiet for a few seconds. And then his shoulders sagged, his face crumpled, and he let out a long breath.

"Some days are okay, and some days I wake up, and I can't believe he is gone. And I want to crawl back under the sheets, stay there and wallow in self-pity."

"It's not self-pity, Aks. Don't be so hard on yourself. Give it time. What you went through was..."

His face tightened as his eyes filled up. The video was clear enough for me to see his jaw clenched tight to stop the tears from spilling out.

"I wish I was there. It hurts to see you like this and not be able to hug you. Stupid video call. Nobody thought of a hug feature? Pathetic technology."

Aks laughed, "I know. I wish you were here too. When this horrid pandemic is over, you have to come and work from here. Or better yet, write from here. Stay with me for a month. No excuses."

"What? Only a month. Oh well, okay. Don't think I can take more than that of you in any case."

"Is this your audition for a stand-up comic? Am I supposed to laugh?" He rolled his eyes. "Hey, it's almost midnight. Ready? Here starts the countdown... Three...two... one... Forty! Happy happy birthday. Welcome to the club."

"Where's my gift?"

"Hello! You are supposed to respond with thank you. Manners, woman!"

"Shut up and tell me where you got mom to hide my gift."

"Join us in the digital world, madam. Check your email. The link to add it to your Kindle has just been delivered to your email."

I tapped open my email on my phone and hit refresh. There it was, Pedro Paramo by Juan Rulfo.

"Ooh, nice. He sounds Spanish or Latin American."

"Yeah. I know your type."

"Don't think I have heard of him, though."

"I read somewhere that Marquez loved this book so much he could recite it backwards and forward. And since you worship Marquez, it is only right that in your old age you be introduced to the one he worshipped, senorita."

"What happened to age is just a number?"

"It is. Just that this one's kind of a big number. Rits, this has to be the decade for you, the writer. Promise me. All three of us are counting on you."

"Three?"

"Me, Marquez and now Juan. Don't let us down. Promise, you won't."

"Okay, okay, I promise. Such a drama queen you are."

"That, my dear, I won't deny. So, how are you celebrating? Are you doing something special with Tara?"

"Yes. I am taking her on a shopping spree to the art shop and then a pizza lunch. Might as well make the most of it while she's at that age where she finds her aunt cool."

"You will always be the cool aunt, even when you are old and doddering."

*****

I sat back in my chair and leaned back. It was half an hour to midnight. It had been a challenge to stay up. Growing old was so bizarre. It was a rare night that I would sleep for a good stretch, and on the one day I wanted to stay awake, the body was adamant about sleeping. Well, too bad, it wasn't happening. There were another twenty minutes to go. I poured myself a cup of coffee from the French press and settled back into my chair.

I knew I was being stubborn about traditions. What was even there to celebrate now? Most body parts were creaking, and others had either stopped working or had been boosted by titanium.

At ten minutes to twelve, the phone rang.

"Happy seventieth birthday!" Tara's voice rang out across the distances.

"Thank you. But I would have preferred it without the proclamation of the number."

"I know. That's why I said it," she giggled.

"It's time to stop being a brat. You are almost 40-yourself."

"Let's focus on your age today, old woman. So, I know I have called ten minutes early, but that's because I need you to do something."

"What?"

"On your bookshelf, look behind the Malory Towers book set."

"What have you planned?"

"Just do it."

"Give me a minute. Old bones, remember."

With my free hand, I moved the faded set of the six books on the lowest shelf. A wrapped package peeked out at me.

"What's this?" I said into the phone and settled back into my chair with the package in my lap. "When did you put this here?"

"A month ago when I was in Bombay. I was quite certain you would not be reading Malory Towers anytime soon."

"Silly girl. I am too old for gifts."

"I agree. That's why it's not from me. It is from Aks Uncle."

"Aks? But… when?"

"He couriered it to me a couple of months before he…»

"And you kept it all these months?"

"His instructions were very precise that you should open it on your birthday eve. So, happy birthday once again. I love you, even though you are an old woman."

"And I love you even though you are a cheeky brat."

"Enjoy your gift."

I hung up and stared at the package in front of me. Trust you to plan this. His photograph among the frames on my desk was looking at me. It was on the beach in Goa a couple of days before my thirtieth birthday. He had pushed his Ray-Bans to his forehead and was squinting at the camera.

"Rits, the sun's behind me. The light is going to be terrible. You should take it from there," he had pointed in the opposite direction as I was adjusting the camera.

"Just shut up and smile. You don't have to control everything."

You do have to control everything, don't you? I looked away from his picture, took a deep breath and unwrapped the parcel. It was a sheaf of papers tied together with a piece of twine. I flipped through them. They were white. Blank. I flipped through them again, and a folded sheet slipped out. It was a note in Aks' hand.

Rits,

Remember you said you would write your book in your ripe, old age. Well, guess what, hon? You are old. And if you wait to ripen anymore, you'll turn rotten. So start writing.

Love you...

P.S. You can dedicate the book to me.

CPSIA information can be obtained
at www.ICGtesting.com
Printed in the USA
BVHW080134210721
612415BV00008B/578